FOUR

UNPOSTED

LETTERS

TO

CATHERINE

*The Word "Woman" and Other
Related Writings*

Selected Poems: In Five Sets

*The Poems of Laura Riding: A New Edition
of the 1938 Collection*

*First Awakenings: The Early Poems
of Laura Riding*

FOUR
UNPOSTED
LETTERS
TO
CATHERINE

LAURA
RIDING

POSTSCRIPT BY
LAURA (RIDING) JACKSON

—

AFTERWORD BY
ELIZABETH FRIEDMANN
AND ALAN J. CLARK

PERSEA BOOKS
NEW YORK

Persea Books, Inc.
60 Madison Avenue
New York, New York 10010

Library of Congress Cataloging-in-Publication Data

Riding, Laura, 1901–
Four unposted letters to Catherine / by Laura Riding.
p. cm.
ISBN 0-89255-192-5
1. Young women—Conduct of life. 2. Jackson, Laura (Riding),
1901–. —Correspondence. 3 Poets, American—20th century—
Correspondence. I. Title.
PS3519.A363F58 1993
811'.52—dc20
[B]   93-3467

Set in Cheltenham Light by ComCom, Allentown, Pennsylvania
Printed on acid-free, recycled paper by The Haddon Craftsmen,
Scranton, Pennsylvania
Jacket printed by Lynn Art, New York, New York

First Edition

CONTENTS

Dear Gertrude.

*The function of Opinion is to be that which
does not get posted. Hating Opinion and
loving All That Gets Posted as you do, you
must applaud my not posting these letters,
however you deplore my writing them.*

Love,

Laura

THE FIRST LETTER

TO

BEGIN WITH

Dear Catherine,

Do you remember the time you asked me about policemen? And I told you about policemen? And when I had finished you said: "Do you know, Laura, sometimes I know everything about everything too?"

When I told you about policemen you did not say "How do you know that?" or "Where did you learn that?" You believed me. And you believed me because I told you what I thought about policemen. I told you why I thought that they were good and why I thought that they were

———

11

bad. I did not tell you that in New York police-
men carried clubs or that in France policemen
wore capes. If I had told you things like that
instead of what I thought, you would not have
believed me. You would have thought that I was
telling you a story.

Yes, I too know everything about every-
thing. But only, of course, if I stop to think about
it—only sometimes, like you, though more often,
of course. You are only a little girl, and so when
you stop to think it is more often to think about
yourself than about everything. But as you grow
up you will get to know yourself so well that you
will not have to stop to think about it at all. You
will just be yourself all the time and sometimes
stop to think about everything. And if you really
are yourself all the time, when you do stop to
think about everything you will certainly know
everything about it—as you do now, only more

---

*often. For if you know everything about yourself,
then you are so clear and bright that you light up
everything around you. And when you stop to
look at it you naturally see everything there is to
see about it.*

*The good thing about children is that if no-
one interferes with them they do stop to think
about themselves. Childhood is the time when
people should be bothered with nothing but
themselves. After childhood there is a time between childhood and grown-up-hood called
adolescence, just before you begin frequently
knowing everything about everything. It is a
rather awkward time because people treat you
sometimes like a child and sometimes like a
grown-up, and you yourself are not sure which
you are. I think the best way out of it is not to
worry which you are, but to be yourself, and then
it will not matter how people treat you. For if you*

---

are yourself being yourself or being a grown-up is all the same thing as far as you yourself are concerned. A grown-up who doesn't first know everything about himself can't know everything about everything. And even if a grown-up does know everything about everything, the important thing is knowing everything about oneself, because that is where knowing everything about everything must begin from.

The trouble is that people interfere with children—not because people are wicked but because of the way of the world. The way of the world is to do a lot of unnecessary things. And so there is less time than there should be—I mean less laziness. And so children are hurried along and made to grow up and start doing things before they really start doing things, that is, before they have finished with knowing about themselves. And so there are a great many

---

14

grown-ups who don't know everything about themselves. And so they do not light up every-thing around them. And so, however well they may do things, it is as if they did them in a dim light. They do things hurriedly and blurredly in order to seem to be people, though not definite people. And so, dear Catherine, it is the world it is.

A child should be allowed to take as long as she needs for knowing everything about herself, which is the same as learning to be herself. Even twenty-five years if necessary, or even forever. And it wouldn't matter if doing things got delayed, because nothing is really important but being oneself. People may call you a lazy girl, and so you are, and so you should be. You do less than the other children, you take longer to do things than they do, you are not clever at carpentering like David or at sewing like Jenny

---

or at drawing like Sam. You seem to spend a lot of time dreaming about nothing at all. And yet you are, as the few people who really know you recognise, a perfect child; even the other children admit this and are not jealous of you. And this is because when you seem to be dreaming about nothing at all you are not being lazy but thinking about yourself. And so you get to be yourself. One doesn't say you are lazy or selfish. If a person is herself she can't be a bad person in any way; she is always a good person in her own way. For instance, you are very affectionate, but that's because you are a good person. You are not a good person just because you are affectionate. It wouldn't matter if you weren't affectionate, because you are a good person. You are yourself, and whatever you do is sure to be good.

It is very sad then that so many children are hurried along and not given time to think about

---

16

themselves. People say to them when they think that they have been playing long enough: "You are no longer a child. You must begin to do something." But although playing is doing nothing, you are really doing something when you play; you are thinking about yourself. Many children play in the wrong way. They make work out of play. They not only seem to be doing something, they really are doing something. They are imitating the grown-ups around them who are always doing as much instead of as little as possible. And they are often encouraged to play in this way by grown-ups. And they are not learning to be themselves.

By this I don't mean that children should do nothing. In fact, I think it would be a very good idea to let children do a great deal of work, if not all the work. For they would do it like play, they would be thinking about themselves all the time,

---

they would only seem to be doing something, they would get the work done without being exhausted by it. They would not be taking work seriously, the way grown-ups are inclined to: grown-ups often get knowing everything about everything mixed up with doing things.

Knowing everything about everything is being yourself and also, because you belong to everything, being everything as well. People are by themselves in being themselves, but together with everyone and everything else in being everything. And this is what makes a world, and people in it. Things that don't think about themselves aren't people; they are just everything. And by themselves they are nothing. And even all together, as everything, they are nothing because they know nothing about everything. We are something because we think about ourselves. And being part of everything we think

---

about everything too and make something of it.

But I was intending to explain to you how grown-ups were inclined to get knowing everything about everything mixed up with doing things. But I think this had better wait for another time. It is much more important for you to play than to go on listening to me.

THE SECOND LETTER

TO CONTINUE

TO BEGIN

WITH

Dear Catherine,

As I explained in the first letter, there are many people who are not entirely themselves because as children they were not given time to think about themselves. And because they don't know everything about themselves they can't know everything about everything. But no one likes to admit that she doesn't know everything about everything. And so these people try to make up for not knowing everything about everything by doing things.

I must try to explain about doing. When the

sun shines, when the wind blows, when you breathe or see things or walk or sit down or sleep—this is doing. Your whole body is doing. The body part of everything is doing. The whole world is doing. The very first thing you are, before you are yourself, is just a doing. And you must be this doing, this body part of you, before you can be yourself. You must feel this doing, this body part of you, before you can begin to think. It is like looking at the binding of a book, reading the title, finding out who wrote it, seeing what it is like generally, before beginning to read it actually.

People who for some reason find it impossible to think about themselves, and so really be themselves, try to make up for not thinking with doing. They try to pretend that doing is thinking. They fight or find out about the spots on the sun or invent aeroplanes or pray to God, and they

———

work very hard, and they become great soldiers or great scientists or great inventors or great saints. I don't mean things that people do together to make life comfortable for everyone or that a person does by herself to make life comfortable for herself, or that people do together to have fun together, or that a person does by herself to have fun by herself. That kind of doing is all right because it makes happily sure of the body part of you and encourages you to think about yourself, and then about everything. In a place where only this kind of doing went on there wouldn't be much doing. The important thing would be knowing everything about yourself and knowing everything about everything, and as much time would be made for this as possible. That is, in such a place the object of life would be laziness.

The wrong kind of doing is doing that peo-

———

ple do not do for comfort or fun but in order to prove to themselves and to other people that they are people. Of course, the only kind of people that people of this sort could impress would be people like them, who wished to seem people in a general way although they weren't particularly speaking people. In a place where most of the people were like this the object of life would be busyness. And, dear Catherine, this is the way the world is. Only a small part of the doings in it are done for comfort or fun. The rest is just showing-off. The greatest showers-off and busybodies are men. And so this world is ruled by men, because it is a world not of doing but overdoing. A world of simple doing would need no ruling. It takes really very little doing to keep comfortably and happily alive. We ought not to pay much more attention to doing than to breathing.

All this extra doing interferes, in fact, with comfort and fun and makes a bad kind of laziness instead of a good kind. Good laziness is thinking—knowing about yourself and knowing also about everything when you want to. It is not really laziness, but I like to put it that way to explain that I mean not doing anything. Bad laziness is not thinking, being stupid. You would be surprised to meet great men when they were not doing anything, when they were being lazy. They are the most stupid people that you could imagine. But you would not be surprised if you realized that it didn't take brains to do things. Birds, bees, ants, dogs, trees, earth, the sky—all these and everything do the most marvelous things, but they haven't brains like ours. Never be impressed by what people do, dear Catherine. Doing is only natural. If your opinion is asked about a doing don't praise it merely be-

---

27

cause it is a doing. But decide if it is sensible, if the person or people who did it did it because it was necessary for comfort and fun, or if they did it because they thought that it was great to do things. If they did it to be great, it is not a good thing.

It is very hard of course at first to decide what is a good thing and what is a bad thing. If someone makes a chair with the idea of making something that will be comfortable to sit in and that one will enjoy sitting in because it is comfortable, it will certainly turn out a good chair, or you might say a beautiful chair, or you might say a good doing. Or if someone who has thought with strong laziness and knows everything about herself and so is herself, if someone like this goes on thinking beyond herself, then you may get something good too. If a person knows everything about herself, then she is herself, which is a part of everything. But if she can think further than this, then she can perhaps make that part into a whole, into everything—not just an everything that is everything and anything, but an everything that is herself, or, you might say, an everything that is precious instead of just ordinary. This good thing, this little everything—well, it might be a poem or anything that a thinking might be, and it would be a good thing because it wasn't a doing; and the chair would be a good thing because it was a doing.

The chair was made because of comfort and the fun of being comfortable, and perhaps the idea of this comfort and this fun made the chair-maker enjoy making it, or perhaps he enjoyed making it because he was working comfortably. However it was, this chair is a good chair because it is a doing which is only a doing; because it doesn't pretend to be thinking as well

---

*as doing. For instance, I know two carpenters.
One is called Jenkins and the other is called
Hawkins. Jenkins made me a chair, and Hawkins made me a chair. When Jenkins made me
a chair he just made it. He didn't try to show off
what a good carpenter he was, he didn't try to
make the chair say, when it was finished: "The
man who made this chair had wonderful
brains." When he made it he simply said to himself: "I will make a comfortable chair for Laura."
And it turned out a very good chair. Then Hawkins made me a chair. And he tried to show off.
He said to himself: "I will show Miss Riding what
a clever fellow I am." And he put little knobs
here and there, and used up all his energy in
making the chair fussy, and the result was an
ugly and uncomfortable chair that made me mis-
erable to sit in.*

As for a poem or anything like that that is

---

thinking and not doing, it is of course much harder work than making a chair, but it is work done with laziness not with busyness. By this I mean that in making a poem there is no hurry or purpose as there is in making a chair; it has nothing to do with fun or comfort, it is better than fun or comfort. Having fun and being comfort-able is connected with being alive for a good long time, a year or maybe a hundred years. But making a poem is like being alive for always: this is what I mean by laziness and there being no hurry or purpose. A good poem, then, or any good thinking thing, wouldn't try to give comfort or fun to people: it would be good because of what it was, not because of what it did, and so give people something better than comfort or fun —a feeling of laziness, of being alive for always. Only someone who was herself in an everything way could make such a thing, but to make such a thing is nothing to be proud of or show off about. For if you are able to make a poem, it doesn't seem a wonderful thing to do; it seems just a necessary-natural thing to do.

But there is a kind of poem you can call a Hawkins poem as there is a kind of chair you can call a Hawkins chair, and the object of both is to get praise, which is the confidence in yourself that you get from people whom you have succeeded in pleasing when you haven't any confidence in yourself. The Hawkins poem is an extraordinary poem, as the Hawkins chair is an extraordinary chair, and the maker in each case is not good enough to make what he's trying to make, and so it is an extraordinary poem or an extraordinary chair when you think who made it, but just a bad one when you don't. If someone makes a good chair you shouldn't praise him, because if it is a good chair it was natural to him

———

to make a good chair. You shouldn't praise him for making a good chair any more than you should blame him for making a good chair instead of a good poem. A person might indeed be able to make both, but they wouldn't have anything to do with each other. It wouldn't be a case of choosing between them, as if in a hurry, but of letting happen what happened naturally, in a slow, unworried way. A person might be able to make a good chair, but she might never have stopped to think about herself, and so on; but making the chair wouldn't prevent her from stopping to think about herself, and so on. Or she might be able to make a good chair and she might also know everything about herself and even sometimes know everything about everything, without happening to turn the two kinds of knowing into one. Or a person might be able to make poems but be unable to make chairs, not because she could only make poems, but because it didn't happen to her to make chairs. In the long run a person who could make good poems would certainly come round to making good chairs, and the other way round. Indeed, it is behaving as if there were only a little time to behave in that causes Hawkins poems and Hawkins chairs to be made. A Hawkins chair is one that tries to combine doing and thinking, as a Hawkins poem is one that tries to combine thinking and doing. And they are each in its way an object-lesson in over-doing: a Hawkins chair shows what happens to simple doing when it comes under the influence of over-doing, as a Hawkins poem shows what over-doing looks like as thinking.

It may seem hard at first to tell the difference between a good thing and a bad thing, but it is really quite easy when you understand the dif-

ference between doing and thinking. Then you see that a thing which is all doing, like a Jenkins chair, is a good thing, and a thing which is all thinking is a good thing—as if it happened to Jenkins, who doesn't mix thinking with doing, to make a poem. You see that the good poem and the good chair are the same in being good but different because thinking is different from doing; but that a bad chair and a bad poem are the same thing, a not-one-thing-or-the-other, a thing that you can't like either as a thinking or a doing, or that is, you might say simply, an un-likeable thing. When a thing is not likeable, that is the end of it. It doesn't matter what it should have been; there's no more to be said about it. And when a thing is likeable it is what it should be, and there's no more to be said about it either.

THE
THIRD
LETTER

TO

DISCUSS
LEARNING

Dear Catherine,

There are two things to understand about learning: one, that it is not real; two, that it can be of some good use only if people remember that it is not real. Learning is the doing side of your mind. When you learn to recite the counties of England or that the Hittites were a strong somewhat barbarous people who once conquered Egypt, then your mind is behaving as if it were your body. It is like making chairs but not so good as making chairs, because when you are making chairs you are really making them.

———

39

Learning is not doing, it is only like doing. And the pity of it is that people often do not know where to stop in learning. When you are really doing things you know where to stop because you get tired when your body has used up all the doing in it: if you go on after you have become tired, you do badly. But with learning it is differ- ent. For, since it is only learning and not really doing, people do not get tired, and so go on and on, and learn more and more, not only the coun- ties of England and about the Hittites, but what the sun is made of and the way to stay up in the air, and so on. And indeed there is no limit to what people can learn if they want to. It is the easiest thing possible. It is easier than doing and it is easier than thinking. It is not real.

Well, then, what is the good of learning? The good of learning is this: that it can cheer up doing that is real doing, just as if you had to peel

---

potatoes a great deal it would be a relief to shell peas. But with learning you do not even shell the peas, you just pretend, so that you don't get tired as you would if you really did shell peas, although you don't get the real pleasure of really shelling peas after you have been really peeling potatoes. Another good thing about learning is this: that it can give you a good idea of all kinds of doing in case for some reason you have a poor idea of doing. And by giving you this idea of doing it can perhaps make you feel the doing side of yourself so strongly that you may say to yourself: "I understand now what it is to make a chair, or to be Hittites conquering, or Egyptians conquered, that is, I feel more definitely what being alive is, and so I can give myself up more freely to thinking, which I do more freely than doing." And this is a very good use of learning if you are the sort of person to whom thinking is

---

more natural than doing or who at any rate doesn't want to do a lot of doing in order to feel more definitely what being alive is. On the other hand, a person might get a more definite feeling of what being alive is in really doing than in just learning. She might go on and on learning and never be able to stop, or she might deceive herself that learning was thinking because it was not doing. Or she might fall in love with learning just because it seemed to be doing and because it made her feel not so much wise as strong. Still, we must not say that learning is of no use at all.

But as everywhere around you you will find people believing that learning is both wise and strong, you have to be careful. You have to avoid learning what people think wise and strong, and learn only what you feel like learning, which will turn out, probably, to be what is helpful to you; or if it is not helpful it will not matter. And there is of course plenty to choose from; because, since it is impossible for people to be learned in absolutely everything, those who believe in the importance of learning choose special branches of learning, to be learned in absolutely everything connected with them. And when at first you look about you and see thousands and thousands of people being importantly learned in this or this or this or this, and each learning a whole different learning by itself, and that all these people are in earnest and not fooling and work hard and when you meet them often have grey hair— well, naturally you are bewildered and do not know where to turn. And you want to be nice and good and to satisfy all of them, and perhaps you try to. But you can't begin everywhere. So you begin somewhere. You might begin at the Romans, or at butterflies, or at electricity. And there you stay stuck. So, dear Catherine, you

——

43

must be careful to satisfy no one but yourself and to look upon learning not as something that it is wise and strong and nice and good of you to do, but as something that you may do if you like but that, in the end, no matter how important it may seem while you are doing it, will make very little difference to what you really do and what you really think.

And you should also keep in mind that the people who are the learners can never come to any end while they are learning. That is, the result of learning is not knowing, whether a person learns old things that other people have learned before him, or whether he learns new things, for other people to learn after him. Learning whether new or old is only learning. And so it does not matter what you learn: an old fact is as good as a new one, and a little is as good as a great deal. It all depends on its helpfulness to *you. And no matter how helpful it may seem you must always remember that you could have got on very well without it—in the long run, of course, which is the only run that matters.*

Still, as I said, learning can be helpful. And besides the ways that I have already shown, it can be helpful in even other ways. For instance, if a person is more inclined to doing than to thinking, if a person is so inclined to doing that she finds it difficult to get away from doing to thinking, if a person, that is, instead of knowing herself, continually prevents herself from knowing herself by inventing jobs for herself to keep her mind off herself, then learning can be helpful in winning her away from doing, for learning seems like doing but is not really doing. Learning can teach her laziness, and laziness can teach her to think. So learning can be a bridge between doing and thinking. But then there is a

—

danger that the person who uses learning as a bridge between doing and thinking may get stuck in learning and never get on to thinking: she may mistake learning for thinking because it is not really doing. Always remember that learning is a bridge between doing and thinking, that it is nothing in itself and that it has no meaning, that is, no value, either as doing or thinking.

Learning is a doing that does nothing, or a thinking that thinks nothing, whichever way you like to put it. It is not being alive and it is not being yourself. It is between the two. And so it is good because it makes it clear that there are the two different things doing and thinking. And so it can also be bad because it can be wrongly understood as a mixture of doing and thinking and wrongly considered better than either doing or thinking by itself, and so wrongly urged upon people as the best possible thing that they can

———

occupy themselves with—when the truth is that learning is nothing at all. It is just fancy. It is just laziness from which nothing can come. I must explain the difference between learning-laziness and thinking-laziness. Learning-laziness repeats what already is. It is a person being everything except herself, a person roaming idly about everywhere. Thinking-laziness is a person being herself, a person roaming idly about herself. The odd part of it is that you get to know everything about everything not from roaming idly about everywhere but from roaming idly about yourself. For the only everything that you can know about is the one that you find in yourself, by knowing yourself entirely and so as its seed.

With learning everything is old. With yourself everything is new. Even if you learn something quite new quite by yourself, for instance, if you learn that it is possible to get from London to Tahiti, which is an island in the Pacific Ocean, in one second by chewing the leaf of a certain plant that blooms only one day every five years in Spitzbergen, which is an island in the Arctic Ocean—even if you learn, that is, find out, something quite new like this that no one has ever learned or found out before you, still it is nothing new or remarkable. It is not knowing anything by thinking. It is roaming idly about everywhere and repeating something already there, finding something possible that is already possible, not making something possible yourself. It is not knowing everything about everything. It is borrowing or even stealing something and pretending that it is your doing or your thinking, when it is really nothing and nobody's— that is, merely something already there for which no one ought to be praised or blamed. It is just learning. Or, you can say, it is just God, meaning not that there is or isn't a God or that God is clever or stupid or good or bad; but meaning that here is this, that and everything else, and that you are not responsible for them one way or the other, and that however learnedly you roam and idle about in this God-world of everywhere, it can amount to nothing important, only perhaps to something helpful, or even perhaps to something not helpful but rather hindering.

From learning-laziness, then, you don't come to know everything: you do nothing and you know nothing about anything, you let things do and know for you. And you really aren't, and they really aren't. Now, what about thinking-laziness? From thinking-laziness, which is roaming idly in and all about yourself, you come to know everything about yourself. And this is not repeating old things but being something new, something that cannot be repeated, something that is yourself as long as you can be it and after that nothing else at any rate. And if you can really be yourself, then everything can be as newly true as you are because of you—providing, of course, that being yourself comes so easily to you that you have a lot of being to give away. This must all sound very complicated to you, dear Catherine, but naturally things sound complicated if you try to explain them, when the reason why you are explaining them is that they ought to be simple but aren't, having got so complicated as to need a complicated explanation to explain how simple they ought to be.

THE FOURTH LETTER

TO

TELL ABOUT THE MUDDLE

I am telling you about the muddle: that is why what I am telling you seems muddled, of course. But once you know that there is a muddle it is easy to be simple yourself. The trouble is that scarcely anyone will admit (least of all to children) that there is a muddle, and so it goes on, without a great many people even knowing about it. A few people, in spite of not being told about it, find out about it by themselves (as you would, only a little less easily than this, however complicated this seems) because they are so easily simple to begin with themselves that they

53

are easily struck with what isn't. Of the others, some are aware of the muddle, and some are not. Some are wicked, that is, and some are stupid. The wicked want the muddle to go on because in some way they profit by it; they are the crooked, or unstraight, or unsimple, people who have power over other crooked people who are not wicked but only stupid. The stupid crooked people, as I said, are not aware of the muddle; they are just anxious to be good—not good in themselves but good meaning being nice, and being nice meaning pleasing the people in charge of things, the wicked crooked, or unstraight, or unsimple people.

Well, you may ask, are all the important people, the people in charge of things, wicked? And I should then answer you something like this. Take any person in charge of things, and you might find that you can like her very much.

Take another, and you may find that you can't like her at all. But liking and not liking have nothing to do with people being wicked and crooked in the way that I mean. Liking people is not like liking chairs or poems. With chairs and poems it means deciding about them, or loving them—if loving was a word to use decidingly about them as well as about people. But with people liking merely means not deciding about them.

And one can easily not decide about others if they don't bother one in any easily named way. Take, then, some person in charge of things. Perhaps you meet her one day, and she smiles, and does not say or do anything that bothers you, and you like her. And that's quite all right. But now think of her at work in the muddle. She knows that things are in a muddle. She might even say that it was too bad that things were in a muddle. But she wouldn't all the same work against the muddle. That is, she doesn't particularly want to be straight because she's not sure whether, if she were, she'd be anything in particular in an unmuddled state of things. She prefers to be an important though anyhow part of things anyhow. And so she goes to work in the muddle, which is caused by people not being their simple selves but just anyhow parts of things anyhow. And she works cleverly and hard and enjoys herself and feels that she's a great fellow. And so she is. And so the muddle goes on, getting more and more muddled.

This is the kind of great fellow that a great man generally is. And this, for instance, is why we still have wars. The straight people can't do anything about it because they are not parts of the anyhow muddle: they belong to a straight way of things. They can only fight against the

---

56

muddle by not being part of it. And of course this can't do much good because the muddle is so big by itself that it doesn't miss them. They can only fight by being straight and saving themselves from the muddle—by setting a good example. And of course the people who are in the muddle don't pay any attention to them. Or when they do pay attention to them, the stupid crooked people confuse them with the wicked crooked people and look on them only as on important people, people with power over other people; while the wicked crooked people, though they know that they are different from themselves, shut their eyes to the difference and to the example. And so the muddle goes on. Sometimes you may even find the straight people trying to do more than set a good example; they may feel it so difficult to be easily simple, because of muddle, that they may try to change it

———

forcibly. But this is generally hopeless; they throw themselves into the muddle, which is so much bigger than they, and they disappear in it; when, if they remained outside, they would at least be noticeable to others like them and make them feel less lonely and uncomfortably odd. It might even be possible to clear up bits of the muddle, if a great many straight people concentrated on a very small part of the muddle. But the only way that the whole muddle can be changed is if the wicked crooked people themselves change, and so the stupid crooked people after them—for these are the muddle.

To come back to the question of liking. You might like a person, and you might say: "As far as I'm concerned, she's a very nice person." And that might be quite true in that way. But all the time she might be a wicked clever person. She might be working with the muddle. And the

---

muddle itself you knew to be always a possible enemy of yours, although you couldn't see her as an enemy when she was in a room with you. This, for instance, is how it would be if a General was a friend of yours. Indeed you might be more likely to like the wicked crooked people than the stupid crooked people, because the wicked crooked people understood about things and, though they were part of the muddle, at any rate knew of the muddle and were what they were quite consciously and by their own decision and not like the stupid crooked people made what they were by other people. You might like a wicked crooked person although he was quite open about his wickedness and crookedness; or although he was a hypocrite about his wickedness and crookedness; or you might like a stupid crooked person in spite of everything. You might even like a wicked crooked person or a stupid

---

59

crooked person better than a straight person. He might happen to have something extraordinarily nice about him that all the straight people that you knew happened not to have—say a kind of laugh. But liking doesn't prove anything one way or the other. The important thing is first to be straight yourself and to know a muddle when you come into contact with one, in order not to be drawn into it. Or, you might say, it is all one thing, being straight yourself and letting nothing interfere.

Here again liking comes in. You might like a wicked crooked person because taking him by himself he didn't interfere with your being straight, although he wasn't straight himself, but you would know at the same time that, taking him with the whole muddle of things of which he was a part, he was in fact interfering with you, and that as such you could not possibly like

———

him. He might even be so greatly wicked and crooked, such a powerful part of the muddle (like Napoleon, for instance), that you couldn't take him by himself and so couldn't like him at all. Anyway liking does not matter, or, at any rate, though it is pleasant to like people where possible, the important thing is to be straight. And by straight I mean straight not in comparison with the muddle that most people and the things connected with them are in, but straight by oneself, without thinking of anyone or anything else.

Knowing about the muddle comes into the question in this way. You must know about it generally of course in order not to be innocently caught up in it, as a great many not easily simple people are. You must know about it you might say in order not to know about it, in order not to allow it to interfere with your being straight your-

---

self should an occasion arise when it might if you didn't know about it. And here you are at the very reason why I have been writing these letters to you: I want to let you know generally that there is a muddle so that you won't depend on anything beside yourself to help you be straight yourself, in case that should be difficult at any time—not even on me. But being straightly yourself ought to be a very easy thing for you to do in spite of the muddle, especially if you know about the muddle soon enough. And I'm writing like this not because I think you need to be written to like this, but because of that "especially if"; which really means, I suppose, that I'm writing like this more for my sake than for yours, because knowing about the muddle is irritating, while writing to you reminds me how knowing about it can be a protection against it and so amusing rather than irritating.

———

This brings us round to learning again. You remember that a little way back I said that you got to know everything about everything not from roaming idly about everywhere but from roaming idly about yourself. That is, people get wisdom from thinking, not from learning, and thinking is just being yourself. And when you are yourself as much as you can be, then you know all about as much as yourself is. And when you know all about yourself, then you can easily know all about everything merely by keeping on thinking: knowing all about everything is being yourself over and over on and on as if forever, so that yourself is like one day of everything, and so as good as everything when it comes to the question of knowing everything about everything. In my first letter I think that I said that if you knew all about yourself you were like a bright light that lit up other things. Well, just as a light shines

---

outside of itself, so thinking is not locked up in a brain. Thinking can go beyond a person, and since a person is her thinking, a person can be more than she seems when you look at her as a person. Indeed there is no limit to what a person can be, that is, there is no limit to thinking. So we can put the whole thing like this: knowing everything about yourself is thinking building itself up, training itself, making itself strong, sure, exact, independent of the brain that you might say is like a nest for it in the beginning: and knowing everything about everything is thinking grown-up, thinking not only being thinking but thinking thinking.

But what of learning? Learning in the sense of being all there is to know is the imitation thinking people do all together who cannot think by themselves—people, that is, who cannot really think. Learning in this sense is not knowing

---

everything about everything, but only knowing everything about this and everything about that; it is not knowing everything about everything, but only knowing everything about the muddle. Nor can the muddle be straightened out by knowing more and more about this and that. Knowing more and more about this and that only increases the muddle. A muddle is people not each straight in herself banding together and believing they can be each straight in herself by being banded together. Learning is like this, making cities and nations of people's minds— making an important muddle of what had been better left as unimportant nature. And people with poor minds therefore love learning: it gives them an air of being superior creatures, when really they are only inferior creatures—confused nature instead of simple thinking nature or simple not-thinking nature.

And what is nature?

Nature is what you don't have to trouble about. It looks after itself. It is everything. Or you might just as well say it is nothing. No matter what you didn't do it would still be there. It's what you don't do about and it's what you don't think about. Or if anyone does, she doesn't deserve any credit for it. Such doing or thinking is only learning; it is what is there anyway. To make learning of it is to try to make yourself out of nature instead of out of yourself—to make a not real doing or thinking. The chief point is that nature is not really, and cannot really be made into, doing or thinking. Nature is just nature. You can say if you like that it is unimportant, or you can say that it is important. It doesn't matter which you say, because it makes no difference. Nature is what is there, regardless of what you

---

say or don't say. If you like you can forget all about it. You can treat it as if it weren't there. Indeed, if you are occupied in being yourself, it isn't there. On the other hand, if you want to relax from yourself, you can rely on its being there to relax into. And you can always shake yourself out of it again, and it won't have made any difference one way or the other, for or against you, or for or against nature.

Nature you might say is the muddle that comes of anything being at all. But it is different from the muddle that people create by not being straight themselves. It is a muddle that doesn't prevent anything. It is only a muddle because it is always a beginning of things. The other muddle is a preventing muddle. It interferes with people being straight themselves. It is a muddle not of a beginning of things but of

---

a middle of things. Things that never stir out of nature, that neither do or think in the way a person can do or think—such things can be a muddle without its being a wrong muddle: they are fresh, they are at the beginning, they haven't really started out on their own. But when things (people, say, this time) start out on their own and then don't carry their job through because they have tackled a job bigger than their size where they would be sure to find others like them who were afraid of tackling their own-sized job alone; and of course stop on the way and of course get mixed up with the other people who stop on the way; then you have a really wrong muddle. And this muddle is a sort of stale nature because it is neither a beginning nor an end. It is history.

And on the word history, dear Catherine, I

———

must close, it being to me the most discouraging word that I know. And perhaps it is that to you, or I have made it so. Not that my object in writing these letters has been to discourage you. But it certainly has not been to cheer you up: any more than when I told you about policemen I described what they wore in different parts of the world. Or perhaps I do not mean so much discouraging as dull. And if, dear Catherine, after carefully avoiding the use in an important way of any word that I hadn't carefully prepared you for beforehand—if then, dear Catherine, I come to the most discouraging or the dullest word that I know, why, it is the best possible word for me to close on. For I can be sure that, if I have done nothing else, I have at least not cheered you up or interested you. And whatever else my intentions may have been in writing these letters to

---

you, these were not among them. And so, how-
ever else I may have failed, I have at least not
succeeded in doing anything that I did not mean
to do.

Love,
LAURA.

POSTSCRIPT

This postscript, written thirty and several years after the letters, is addressed to Nobody In Particular instead of to A Particular Somebody. The child to whom I addressed them has dissolved into A Person Unknown. Let us say that the postscript is addressed to Persons Unknown. But I the writer of the postscript ought also to be described as A Person Unknown, as compared with the writer of the letters. For I would say many things said in them differently, now, and some things there said

---

I'd not say at all, now—and I'd say some different things. Indeed, I'd probably not write such letters to a child, now, or to a grown-up, even—such easy-speaking letters, treating with so much diffident good-humor the stupendous, incessantly-urgent matter of Virtue and the lack of it.

When I wrote the letters, I thought that Virtue—by which I mean the eternal virtue of good Being, not the mortal virtue of good Custom—was much better loved, where looked upon with favor, than later experience showed it to be. And so, in taking Virtue for my subject, I made myself cosier than was warranted. I softened my seriousness as one avoids pressing points hard with people presumed to be already sympathetic—of course, I was writing not just for the single child but for people who might have a child like that in their spirit. There

———

74

was much more necessity for pressing points hard in the matter of Virtue than I allowed for in the letters. And so it was also with everything else I wrote, including my poems, in the days of my first understanding of things.

I thought that in my poems I would make up for any easy-goingness in my presentation elsewhere of the case for eternal virtue; and you will see, in the letters, that I held a poem to be an achievement of the highest worth. But in the days of my second understanding of things I became aware that a poem resembles an eternal good only as Sunday-best (in clothes, dinner, behavior) resembles Best. Know, O Persons Unknown of the Present, that when I speak of a poem, in the letters, as an example of the Best, that is only how I *spoke*. As the Person Unknown of the Present I am, I would offer, as the best example of the Best, *natural truth*. That is not making words *sound* good, but, simply, making them be true to the good in you. But I must not get too far ahead of myself here—the myself, I mean, who wrote these letters.

Laura (Riding) Jackson
1963

A FTERWORD

Laura Riding was a widely respected American poet and critic when she wrote these letters to the eight-year-old daughter of her English friends Robert Graves, a fellow writer, and Nancy Nicholson, an artist. She had gone to England in 1926 and there had established, with Robert Graves, the Seizin Press. Among their early publications —all handprinted—was a short work by Gertrude Stein, to whom the epigraph letter here is addressed. By 1930, the year of this book's publication, they had moved their press to Majorca.

Four Unposted Letters to Catherine had, meanwhile, been published by The Hours Press in Paris, in a limited edition of 200 copies, each signed by the author. Its publisher, Nancy Cunard, wrote later that she was at first somewhat puzzled by these letters of Laura Riding's, but that after reading them many times "it seemed to me that

---

her intent was increasingly clear; all was so simply stated, and I had been looking, at first (though why?), for inner meanings."

Laura Riding and Robert Graves remained in Majorca, writing and publishing, until the Spanish Civil War forced their departure. After a time spent in England, Switzerland, and France, Laura Riding returned to America in 1939, and two years later married Schuyler B. Jackson, a poetry editor for *Time* magazine. The Jacksons settled in Florida, and until his death in 1968 were jointly engaged in a comprehensive study of language, seeing language as "the essential moral meeting-ground." Early in the course of this work, Laura (Riding) Jackson came to believe that poetry presents basic obstacles to truthfulness in speaking. She therefore stopped writing poems.

At the request of the British Broadcasting Corporation, she allowed *Four Unposted Letters to Catherine* to be broadcast, on two consecutive days in July, 1963, and provided the preface offered in this edition as a postscript. After her husband's death, Laura (Riding) Jackson completed their book on language, published *The Telling*—her "personal evangel"—in 1972, and continued to write on subjects of general human concern. She died in Florida on September 2, 1991, at the age of ninety.

Much of Laura (Riding) Jackson's early writing has been unavailable until recently (she herself discouraged re-publication of her poems for a time), but her work, poetry and prose, has been praised throughout the twentieth century for its distinctiveness of style and originality of thought.

Elizabeth Friedmann
Alan J. Clark